Hold THE Boat!

JEREMIAH GAMBLE

ILLUSTRATED BY

JOY ALLEN

BETHANY BACKYARD®
www.bethanyhouse.com

2

The sunshine shone across this land;

it was always sunny, always grand.

The forecasters had an easy job.

"Not a cloud in the sky," they'd say with a nod.

But somebody recently ruffled their feathers

when he said we were in for a big change of weather.

3

This man's name was Noah, and he built a great ark

(it's a boat that's real big and is made out of bark).

But everyone here said he was cuckoo and crazy,

said he was loony and loco but certainly not lazy.

He was a hard worker, there wasn't a doubt—

it was his mind everyone wondered about.

He said it was going to rain.

"What's rain?" they all said. "Please explain."

"It's water that falls from way up in the sky."

"Way up in the sky? There's no water that high!"

"Yes, there is," he replied,

"and what's more important,

it's coming back down,

and it's coming in torrents.

So listen, you people, you

women and fellas:

It's too late for you to invent

some umbrellas.

It's going to rain water, and it's

going to rain hard,

and a flood's going to wash

you right out of your yard!"

7

"Boo! Hiss and rubbish," they all replied.

"The forecast looks sunny!" the weatherman cried.

So Noah spun around and returned to his work,

and the people all laughed at this man and his ark.

I wanted to say something—I wanted, but couldn't.

I wanted to tell those who were laughing, they shouldn't.

For I started to believe that the sky might just rain,

and I really didn't want to get washed up and away.

8

So I set out determined to get on his boat
('cause rather than drown, I prefer to be afloat).
I didn't tell anyone, I was somewhat afraid
of what they might think and what they might say.
So I went off alone to find my way there,
and I brought along sunscreen and some swimming wear
(if the boat was too crowded, I'd have to dog paddle—
something I learned from my dog, Fiddle Faddle).
Just all the more reason to ask good ole Noah
and get on his ship and off we would go-ah!

But there was just one small problem—I forgot to explain

only two animals were allowed, two of every name:

Two squirrels, two rabbits, maybe two donkeys,

two lions, two tigers, two yellow-striped bees.

But no people on board, except Noah and his kin,

for they had pleased God and repented of sin.

Everyone else who lived in this land

was selfish and mean, and so out of hand

that God was sending rain to wash more than their chins—

He was sending a great flood to start over again.

So getting on the ark would be kind of a trick,

and I came up with a plan, and I thought of it quick.

14

I walked up to a porcupine, and I saw all its bristles,

so I went to the woods, and I picked out some thistles.

I stuck them on my body, and they looked pretty good,

but they hurt just as badly as you're thinking they would.

15

I went up to a giraffe,
and I measured its height.
I was six inches shorter—
well, okay, not quite!

I behaved like a monkey, and I ate a banana.

(I've been told I have fleas and long hair like my grandpa.)

But I've never been good at swinging from trees—

it's the falling I'm scared of, the climbing's a breeze.

I attached a big stick to my head, like a horn,

and I pranced and I neighed like a small unicorn.

But I never saw any. They never did show.

I guess they got lost—I really don't know.

I slithered like a snake, and I stuck out my tongue,

but I couldn't shed my skin—it stayed where it belonged.

I jumped like a cricket,

but the singing was a chore:

My legs didn't make a sound,

and they got really sore.

25

My friends called me chicken,

'cause I was always afraid

(and I still had my chicken suit

from the play in first grade),

so I put a dozen eggs in the pockets of my pants

and I sat, to keep them warm and away from the ants.

But the eggs didn't last long. They cracked and they split.

(Is there anyone here who wants a giant omelet?)

I roared like a lion,

and I scratched with my feet,

but I needed lots of salt

to stomach the raw meat.

Well, I finally decided to sneak in with the apes.

I walked on my knuckles, my cheeks stuffed with grapes.

30

I made ape-like sounds, and I scratched and I sniffed.

When I caught Noah's eye, he looked kind of miffed.

He pulled me aside, and he asked me my name.

I said, "Ooh-ooh" and grunted, but he was on to my game.

He looked in my eyes, and he squinted his some.

He raised up his hand, and he stuck out his thumb.

He sniffed at the air, and he cracked a small grin.

He said, "Rain's comin' soon. Come on, let's get in."

I let out a sigh, and I spit out my grapes.

He laughed and said, "You're a bit short for an ape.

And I just happen to have room out on the high seas

for two of every animal...

...and one child

who believes."

A NOTE TO PARENTS

Hold the Boat! is a "what if" story based on the account of Noah's ark found in Genesis 6:5–9:17. This picture book should not be read in place of the biblical account, but rather to give young readers a child's-eye view of this story and its timeless message of believing and following God, even when no one else is. We encourage you to read the actual Genesis passage with your child before talking about the following:

1.) Why did God flood the earth?

2.) God told Noah to build the ark so that he and his family could be saved from the flood. Why did God want to save Noah and his family?

3.) God did not save Noah because he was stronger or smarter than other people, but because he obeyed God and did the right thing. If anyone else had been good like Noah, do you think God would have saved that person, too?

4.) In *Hold the Boat!,* the boy hears Noah warn of the coming flood, believes, and chooses to go with Noah and his family—even though no one else thinks the earth will really flood. There will be times in your life when people might make fun of you or try to keep you from doing what is right. What should you do when this happens?

5.) Noah's story took place long ago, but God is still very much a part of people's lives today. It is up to us to choose to say "yes" to God's gift of grace in His Son, Jesus, and, like the boy in the story, follow Him where He leads us. Have you said "yes" to God?